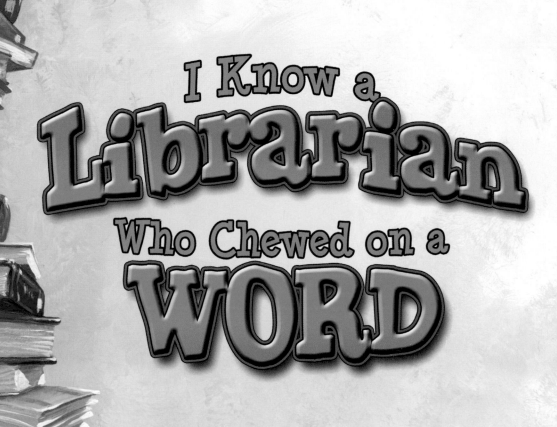

I Know a Librarian Who Chewed on a WORD

I Know a Librarian Who Chewed on a WORD

Written by
Laurie Lazzaro Knowlton

Illustrated by
Herb Leonhard

PELICAN PUBLISHING COMPANY
Gretna 2012

*For J.C. and all the librarians who welcomed me
and my books into their libraries*

*The word "Pelican" and the depiction of a pelican are
trademarks of Pelican Publishing Company, Inc., and are
registered in the U.S. Patent and Trademark Office.*

ISBN 9781589808928

Printed in Singapore

Published by Pelican Publishing Company, Inc.
1000 Burmaster Street, Gretna, Louisiana 70053

I know a librarian who chewed on a word.

She practically purred when she ate that fine word.

How absurd!

Hey! Did you see that? Miss
Devine ate a word!

I know a librarian who swallowed a book.

The red one about old Captain Hook!

She swallowed the book to embrace the word.

She practically purred when she ate that fine word.

How absurd!

Unreal! Miss Devine ate a book!

I know a librarian who ate a book cart, munching and crunching every last part!

She swallowed the cart
to hold the book.

She swallowed the book
to embrace the word.

She practically purred
when she ate that fine
word.

How absurd!

Yowzer! That had to hurt!

The cart, the book, and the word?

Yes!

I know a librarian who
chomped down a chair,
the story-hour chair
that was sitting
right there!

She swallowed the chair to cushion the cart.

She swallowed the cart to hold the book.

She swallowed the book to embrace the word.

She practically purred when she ate that fine word.

How absurd!

No way!

Not the story-hour chair!

The story-hour chair, the cart, the book, and the word?

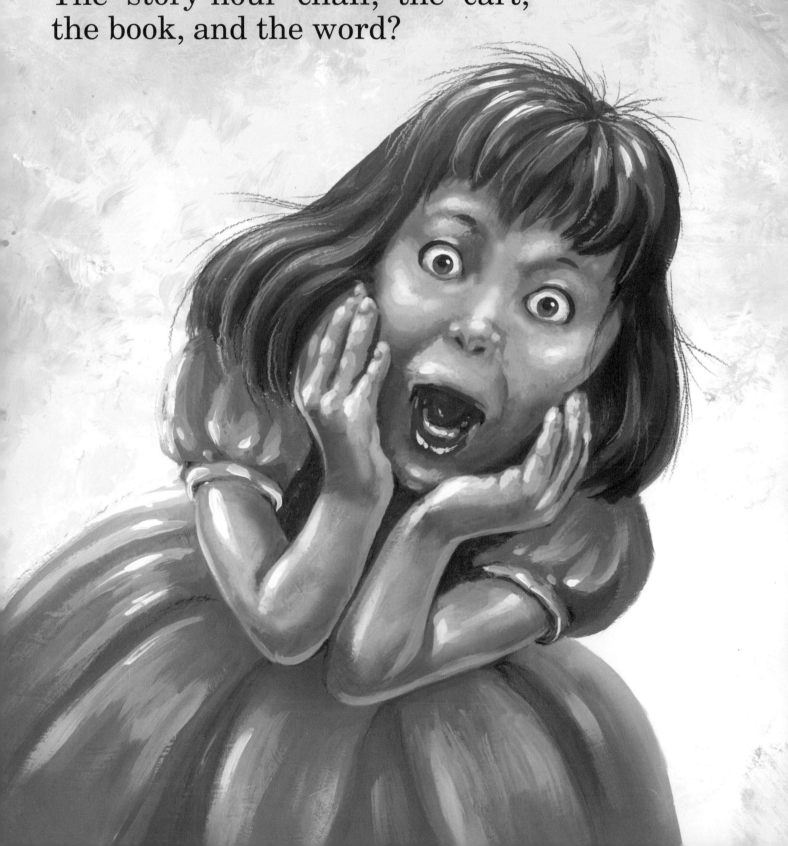

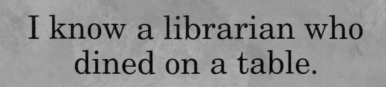

I know a librarian who
dined on a table.

Who'd have thought she'd be
willing and able?

She swallowed the table
to match the chair.

She swallowed the chair
to cushion the cart.

She swallowed the cart to
hold the book.

She swallowed the book to
embrace the word.

She practically purred
when she ate that fine
word.

How absurd!

A whole table?

I saw her with my own two eyes.
She ate the table, the chair, the
cart, the book, and the word.

You saw it?

What's the WORD?

I know a librarian who savored a shelf.

Who'd have thought she could eat it herself?

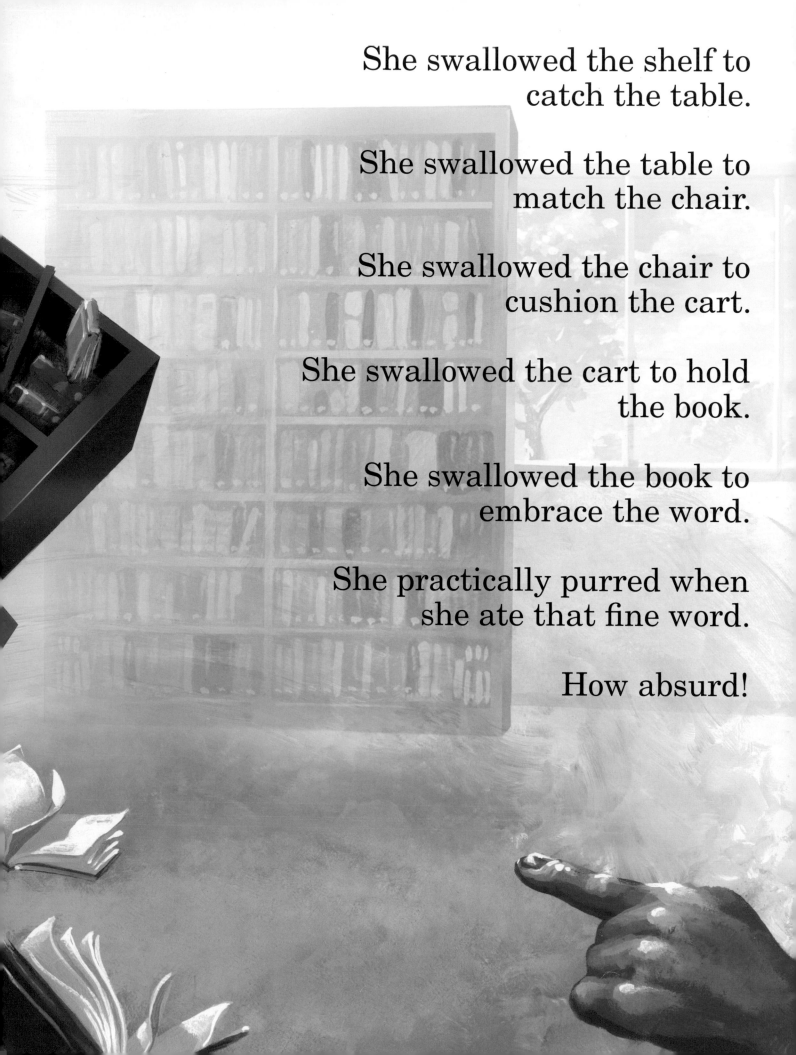

She swallowed the shelf to
catch the table.

She swallowed the table to
match the chair.

She swallowed the chair to
cushion the cart.

She swallowed the cart to hold
the book.

She swallowed the book to
embrace the word.

She practically purred when
she ate that fine word.

How absurd!

Miss Devine just ate the nonfiction bookshelf.

It's gone!

The shelf, the table, the chair, the cart, the book, and the word?

IS THAT WORD?

Then she chomped and chewed,
and we all yaw-whooooed.
Watch out! Watch out! She's
picking up speed!

Then out
popped the
word.

The word was

READ